D1176446

and
the
shrinking
forest

By James W. Dixon III

illustrations by Jem Sullivan

Library of Congress Cataloging-in-Publication Data
Dixon, James W.
ISBN 1-880453-32-0
King Kaneeze and the Shrinking Forest
John Hefty, Hefty Publishing Company®

Dedicated to Peggy
J.W.D.

One day, a child named Jaz met a most unusual dragonfly, who went by the name of Scat.

"Something is very wrong at my home in the prehistoric forest," Scat pleaded. "You must come and help me warn the king!" "But how can I do that?" Jaz asked.

Take a hand full of sand and let it run through your fingers," explained the worried little dragonfly. " Then, carefully study the last grain ... and imagine you can fly like me!"

Jaz did as Scat said. Together, they eyed the last grain of sand very closely. At first, nothing happened. Suddenly, Jaz began swirling into the world of the past, turning into a colorful dragonfly, just like Scat.

After more whirling and twirling, two dizzy dragonflies settled into Scat's homeland.
It was the place where time began . . . in a prehistoric forest of the great dinosaurs!

Jaz and Scat found themselves in the company of a mighty TYRANNOSAURUS REX (tie ran' o sawr' us rex) named King Kaneeze. He was king of the tyrant lizards, and feared by everyone in the forest.

The king was very selfish and lazy. He used up the forest, never replacing what he took.
He even commanded others to destroy the trees just to bring him fresh leaves for his bed.

On this particular day, King Kaneeze slowly raised his sleepy head and looked to the mountains in the distance. "Hmmmm," he grumbled to no one in particular. "The mountains seem to look different today. Could they be growing?"

"Sire," warned Scat, "if the mountains are growing, it could mean danger for everyone!"
The king laughed loudly at the idea, then glared at the two intruders. "YOU are the one i
danger, insect!" roared the king, and he lunged forward with his powerful jaws opened wide.

Both dragonflies frantically fluttered away to safety. "Wow, he sure is mean!" remarked Jaz. "Yes, he is," replied Scat . . . "but we must warn the others about the growing mountains!"

They came upon Bruno BRACHIOSAURUS (brak io sawr' us), busy at work clearing trees for the king.

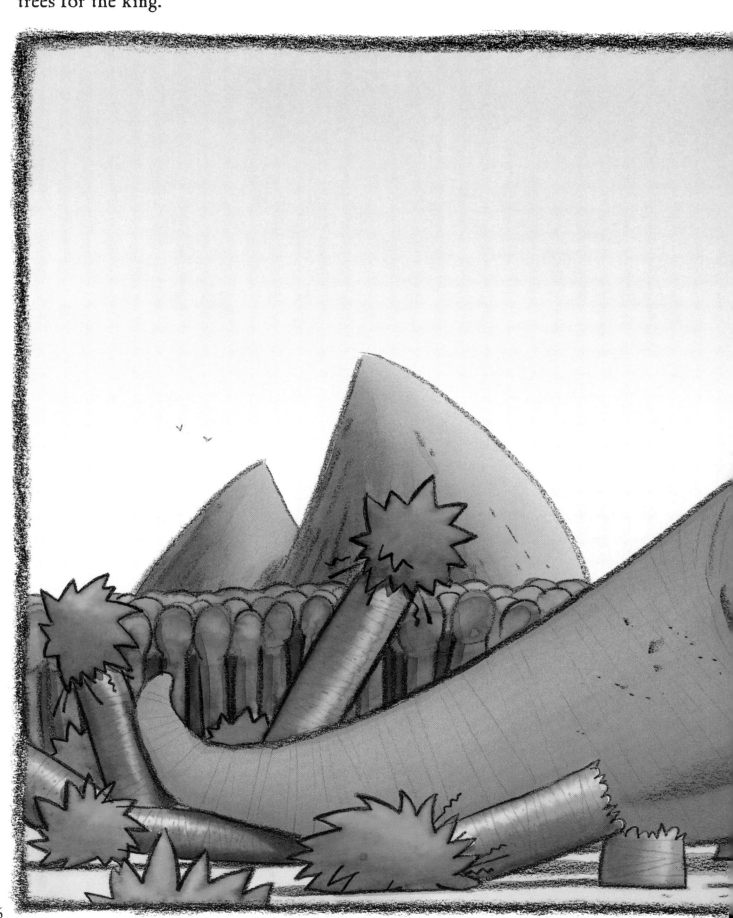

"Bruno!" cried Scat . . . "The mountains are growing and we must find out why!"

FUTURE SITE
of THE KING'S
ROYAL POOL

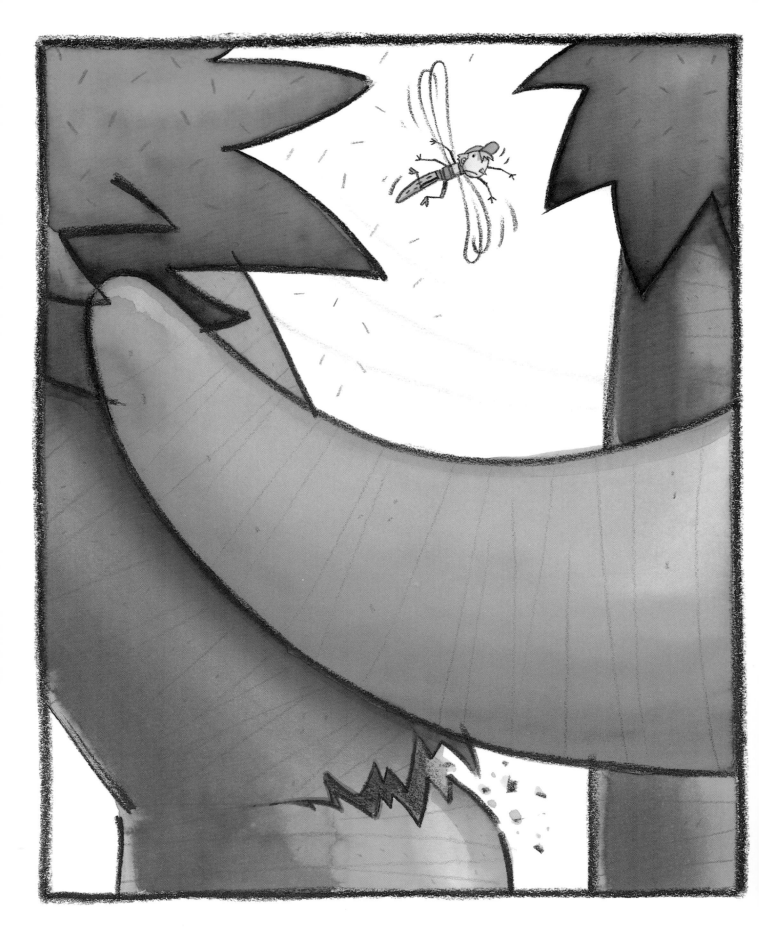

"Go away!" snarled Bruno. "I've got more important things to do." He turned around sharply, almost smashing Jaz with his heavy tail.

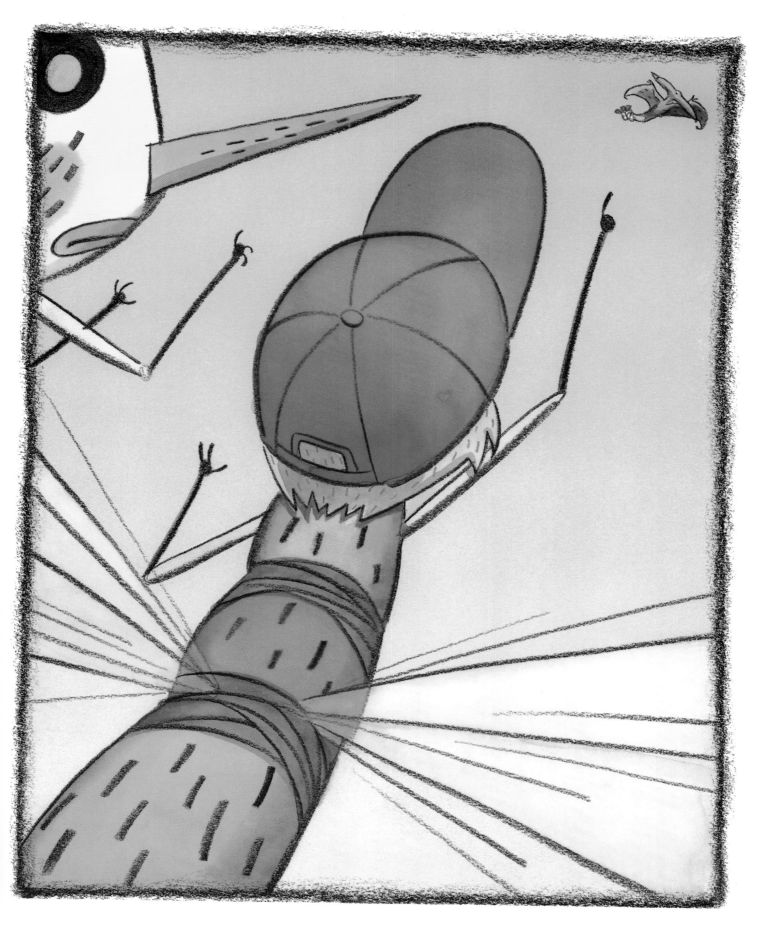

Next, they saw Telly PTERANODON (ter an' o don), the flying reptile. "Telly!" shouted Scat. "Don't you see the mountains are growing?"

"Out of my way!" Telly scoffed. "I'm late for my party." He continued his flight, not even looking up at the mountains. Jaz was concerned that no one seemed to care.

Stella STYRACOSAURUS (sty rak'o sawr' us) was pulling tasty reeds from the marsh. "Please help us warn the others about the growing mountains!" pleaded Jaz. "Go away and let me eat in peace," huffed Stella. She showed no interest in the mountains.

Without warning, King Kaneeze suddenly came crashing through the bushes! He was very angry. "I'll get you trouble makers!" he bellowed. The furious king snatched Scat up into his sharp claws!

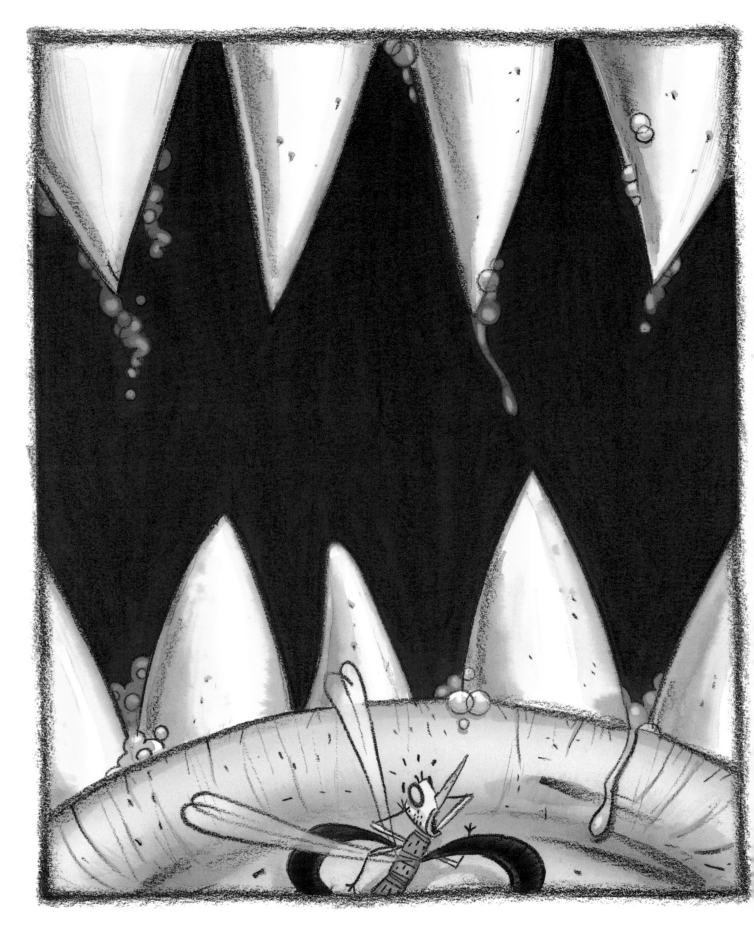

Slowly, the huge beast raised Scat to his big . . . ugly . . . mouth. "Help!" cried Scat. "He's going to eat me! Help! HELP ME!"

Without hesitation or concern for his own safety, Jaz quickly flew up into the king's nose. He flapped his wings wildly, causing the startled king to loosen his grip on Scat.

King Kaneeze dropped to his knees and heaved a mighty sneeze
that shook the leaves from the trees! The resulting breeze hurled
the two helpless dragonflies far from the forest.

Slamming into the mountains, their wings became entangled. Looking down into the valley, Jaz and Scat saw they had been wrong. The mountains were not growing at all. In fact, the entire forest was rapidly shrinking right before their eyes!

"We must go back and tell them!" cried Scat. When Jaz and Scat finally broke free, they flew as fast as they could, but they could not reach the ever-shrinking forest in time. It had simply become too small.

Jaz was left with no choice but to return to his sandbox and become a kid again. Scat thanked his friend for saving his life, and they sadly said goodbye.

Alone, Scat continued on his quest to find his lost home.

While others may wonder what really happened to the creatures of prehistoric time, Jaz remembers the shrinking forest. Now, when he peeks under a leaf or a blade of grass, he hopes to someday catch a glimpse of the dinosaurs and their once fierce King Kaneeze. Perhaps they will never realize just how small they have become.

THE END